T0144030

THE BABY SITTER'S MAGIC MOUSE STORY BOOK

REMEMBERING HARVEY JOB MATUSOW, HILDA TERRY, TEENA, AND DORCAS GOOD

by
hilda terry
and
Job Matusow

To order additional copies of this book, contact:
Xlibris
1-888-795-4274
www.Xlibris.com
Orders@Xlibris.com

Dedicated to
Emily Matusow,
Dorcas Good,
and
Gregory d'Alessio

without whose
loving help,
wizardry and magic,
nothing would ever
have been done

Angelville

It all started a long, long time ago. . .

In a faraway place, close to the
hearts of those loving love, there was a
village called Angelville. If you were going too fast,
or happened to sneeze, you might not see it. Angelville
was a tiny speck of a place; a desert oasis, with simple wooden
and adobe houses and dirt roads.   But the light that shone from
Angelville was so strong, it could be seen as far away as the farthest
star, and its light was like the sparkling tips of the heavens. The only
way one could get to Angelville, was to find the secret path that led to
The Center Of Everything. Now, some say that this path was created
by a tiny, oh so tiny, glob of shimmering magic energy, that lived
high in the heavens above Angelville. It had no shape, nor any
form.———— It was just "it", freely floating in the heavens.
But wherever it went —— it brought love, joy,
peace, happiness, harmony,
and understanding —

which

somehow

brought Angelville

and "The Center Of Everything,

" together with Teenerville,

and *"The Center Of All That."*

The Arrival of Mouse

Then one day, from that faraway place, there came a tiny cry from all the children of Angelville, who had gathered in a circle and looked up to the heavens and said, "PLEASE, whoever you are, whatever you are –will you come to our village—to our planet earth? Please come and teach us to live in harmony and understanding with all living and growing things?"

"Of course I'll come," said the tiny glob of magic energy. "But what form shall I take? Shall I look like you? Or you? Or you? Or who?"

The children looked at one another, somewhat puzzled and confused "We don't know what form you should take. No one knows, but it doesn't make any difference. Just come!" they replied.

The tiny glob thought for a moment, then said, "All right. Then I shall come as a large bird-like creature—so large, so gigantic, that I shall frighten all beings into doing whatever you want, so you can have your wish."

"OH NO!" the children said. "You can't be big and mean and frighten people into doing what we want. If you want someone to do something, you must be gentle and kind. You must be loving and caring and sharing. Don't be large and mean. Be small. Be so tiny that no one will ever see you... Be a mouse. BE A MAGIC MOUSE!"

And in the snapping of a finger, the twinkling of an eye, the deed was done. Magic Mouse arrived in Angelville. The children cheered! They jumped for joy! What a delight! What excitement! Magic Mouse had come to stay!

And in the neighboring town of Teenerville, yet another visitor had come to stay with Teena, "The Center Of All That."

DON'T CRY, LUV.
TEENA'S GONNA READ YOU
SOME NICE STORIES
FROM A NICE BOOK
SO YOU WON'T
HAVE TO WORRY ABOUT
LOSING YOUR PLACE.

Welcome!

The children of Angelville immediately invited Mouse to move into the tree house in Mother Ammal's garden and mouse accepted.

Now Mother Ammal's garden was no ordinary Garden. In fact, each and every flower, tree, plant, herb, and animal in it could speak as well as you and I. There was no better place in all the universe than this light filled garden for a Magic Mouse to make itself at home!

Mouse's tree house was nestled snugly in the branches of Peter Oak Tree, Angelville's wise and dignified Justice of the Trees. As soon as Mouse's light was seen within the tree house and the children were sure ... absolutely, positively, certainly, no mistake about it sure ... that Magic Mouse was there, they began to rush about the village shouting "Magic Mouse is here! Our troubles are over!" OUR TROUBLES ARE OVER!

And Mouse only smiled and said "Perhaps— when they one day understand that sunshine has nothing to do with the weather."

"What's all the fuss about?" asked a confused Mayor Findhorn McDeva as he stepped out of his tinker's wagon.

The children excitedly told him of Magic Mouse's arrival.

"A Magic Mouse, indeed," said the Mayor."If there's a Magic Mouse, where is it? And what does it look like?"

There was a stunned silence in the garden. They had made a terrible mistake. They had asked Mouse to be so small as to never be seen. That meant that no one could tell if Mouse were a boy or a girl.

And Mayor Findhorn McDeva insisted on knowing, for there was no place for recording an "it" in the official records of the Official Committee of Angelville.

Just then, before another word was said, a penny dropped from the sky and hit Mayor McDeva on the head.

"It makes no difference, be I boy or girl," Mouse laughed. "I am just . . .the Magic Mouse."

"How can we tell when you're around?" asked the Mayor. "Isn't it enough that we have one invisible creature in Angelville?"

The Mayor was referring to his dear friend and companion, Really Really, the invisible leprechaun. It was Really Really who had accompanied the Mayor when he first entered Angelville two weeks earlier. Both of them had arrived tired and worn out vagabonds who'd been on the Road of Life forever and were desperately searching for a place to stay.They had discovered Angelville, and it suited them. When they asked for the mayor, they found there was none. And better still, there was no one who even wanted that position.

So Really Really taught the flowers to speak. As soon as they got their voices, they demanded, and got, the vote. Once they got the vote, they had elected Findhorn McDeva as mayor.

The mayor demanded to know if Mouse had anything to do with the penny that fell from the sky, hitting him on the head.

"I have to admit that I am responsible," confessed Mouse. "I'm truly sorry if I hurt you by dropping it on your head. Had you not reacted in anger, the penny would have stuck to your forehead as a signal that Magic Mouse is about."

"Don't be silly," said the mayor. "Pennies don't stick to people's heads."

"They do if you believe," said the mouse, as he scattered a handful of pennies. The children laughed gleefully as they began picking up the pennies and sticking them to their foreheads. shouting WE BELIEVE! WE BELIEVE!

Magic Mouse then shared with them the secret of the penny. "When you take a penny that Mouse has left and put it under your pillow at night, you'll find the penny still there in the morning, but—all your scary dreams will be gone. They may never return unless you allow them to."

Mayor Findhorn McDeva just stood there in amazed silence. He was confused, bewildered and perplexed. How was he,as Mayor of Angelville, going to deal with a Magic Mouse that he could not see. He then excused himself, went into his tinker's wagon, and asked his secretary, The McDeva switchboard, to call a meeting of the Official Committee immediately.

The Official Committee could then adopt an official attitude of official behavior for officials who were officially dealing with Magic Mouse on official business.

Shortly thereafter, all the officials arrived. The meeting was officially called to order and they officially passed an official resolution to officially invite all in the village to an official celebration to officially welcome Magic Mouse to Angelville. As official procedures had to be officially followed in the most official way, it was officially agreed to have the official celebration the next day. The children, on hearing this news were not at all accepting of it.

"What's wrong with now?" they asked. "Magic Mouse is here. We are here. The time is here." Ignoring the Mayor with his official proclamation, they rushed home to ask Mother Ammal if it would be all right to have a party to celebrate Mouse's arrival.

Mother Ammal, being older and wiser, looked at the clock and said "I'm afraid it's too late. The sun is setting. The chores have to be done, dinner served, and bath and study time ... no, I'm afraid it's too late. Why not have your party tomorrow with the Official Committee?"

"Please, please," the children cried. "It's not every day that a Magic Mouse arrives to live in our garden."

"No,"said Mother Ammal firmly. "It's just too late ... it's too late ... too late ...

At which Magic mouse politely interrupted and said, "What if I can get time to stop? If time were to stop, all the clocks in Angelville would stop. Then everyone could go to bed when they were tired, rather than because the clock said so."

"Don't be silly," replied Mother Ammal. "No one has ever stopped time, and no one ever will. We've kept time by the quarters of the moon, the blooming of the flowers, the coming of the birds, the movement of the tides, but — you can't stop time."

"I believe I can," said Magic Mouse. At that moment Father Time came to the garden entrance.

"Excuse me, Mouse. Open the gate, please. I must be on my way."

"Sorry Father Time. We can not give you passage nor right of way , unless —you agree to stop and rest and stay..."

"Don't be silly ," said Father Time. "Time can not stop. Time has never stopped. Time must move on and on and on.

There's wake up time, bath time, breakfast time, school time, work time, lunch time, come home from school time, come home from work time, dinner time, bed time — time for this and time ... Time can not stop. It must move on and on."

"I can teach you." said Mouse.

"You can teach me? Will it take much time? I don't have much time." The children giggled. "Time doesn't have much time! How silly can time be? How silly can Time be?"

And they began dressing for the party in their grown-up play clothes.

"How do I stop, Mouse. How do I stop?" *SIMPLY STOP* ... and when Mouse said that, Time collapsed in a chair and immediately fell asleep . . . and the Time Stop Party began.

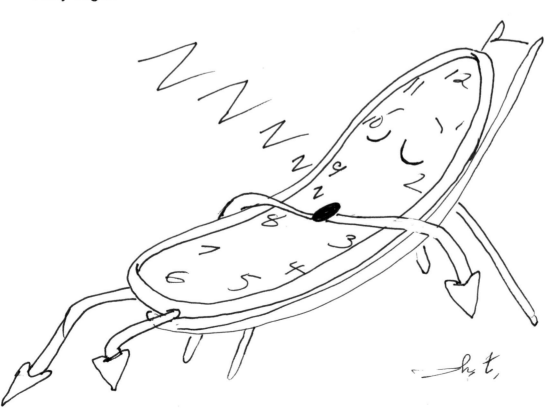

3-31

The Time Stop Party

The Fuzzy Strokers Marching Make Believe Herb Band came in playing a make believe march, and the flakes of Angelville air lifted a giant grand piano to the garden to provide shade for the Fuzzy Strokers Make Believe Band. The children were so happy they rushed over to Mouse and said, "Mouse! Please teach us a game!"

And Mouse said, "When you rushed about before to let people know I was here, what did you do?"

"Well, we shouted. We shouted MAGIC MOUSE IS HERE. OUR TROUBLES ARE OVER!"

"No need to shout," said Mouse. "A truth, whispered, will carry on the wind until the whole world hears it. Besides, did you know when you whisper, you have to smile? And when you whisper with a smile, people will say; Come closer. What did'ja say?"

The children had fun with the game of whispers and smile, so they asked Mouse to teach them another game. Mouse asked, "Well whom among you have been angry?" The children all raised their hands.

"The next time you're angry," Mouse said, "simply go into the garden and sit in silence for an hour with one flower. All your anger will lose its power."

Well, the flowers in Angelville could speak as do you and I, and when they heard that they should tackle all the anger, they said "sit in silence for an hour with a tree, and let your anger go free." And the trees said "Sit in silence for an hour with a friend, and anger will surely end." And the friends said "Sit in silence for an hour with a cat and your anger will lose it's snap." And young Albertina Cuddlewick, the silliest of Mother Ammal's children said "Sit in silence for an hour with an ant. I betcha can't."

The children loved that game, also, so they asked Mouse to teach them again, another. Mouse asked them what they did when they woke up in the morning. Well, they all said they turned on the television and watched the cartoons. Mouse smiled and said "I don't do that. When I wake up, I thank the Lord for another day. Then I run out to play, and say I'd rather be me than watch TV. I think I'll go and hug a tree. I'd rather be me. I'd rather be me, and live a life of simplicity."

The children asked, if you don't watch TV, what else is there to do? And Mouse said, "Well, I can go out and find some wood, and carve it into something good. I'll find a rock and beat the ground, and listen to its drumming sound.

I'll climb a tree, my rocket ship. I'll close my eyes and take a trip. For I'd rather be me than watch TV. I'd rather be free."

After the children learned this game, they began to go to sleep—not because the clock said they must, but because they were tired. And when the last of the children were tucked in, Mouse went over to a sleeping Time and tapped him on the shoulder.

"Time! Time! It's time to get up."

Father Time opened his eyes and as if by magic, they were sitting in a room of all time. On the wall was a huge clock with millions of hands, each one set to every minute of every hour and every second that there ever was, and that there ever will be.

"It's beautiful," said Father Time. "But what is it?"

"This is a time room," Mouse replied. "The key is on your watch chain. It's for everyone who is ever nervous about ever being early or late.
You can let them in to look at your clock; to gaze on the time they want to be at — and if they have made themselves ready, they will be there."

"Thank you Mouse," said Father Time, as he walked down the garden path. "Thank you for teaching me that time is only a product of my anxious mind.

NOW, TIME IS EVERYONE'S PROBLEM~~
But everyone's problem with Time is something else again.

21

The Day of the Dinosaur

Mouse enjoyed the Time Stop Party, thinking it such a gentle balanced way in which to get to know one another. Mouse was happy to be in a village where universal love was so accepted as a natural way of being. All seemed to be of one heart and one mind.

"What an inspiration for a troubled world," thought Mouse. "But is the world ready to receive the message?"

Just as Mouse was having these thoughts, the Deva Switchboard called and said they had a message from Mouse's old friend Tyrannosaurus Rex, the message being that Tyrannosaurus Rex was urgently in need of Magic Mouse and would Mouse drop everything and give first priority to his call?

"It must be important," said Mouse. "This is the first time in fifty four million years he has called. When a dinosaur breaks a fifty four million year silence, one had better believe it's important."

Mouse immediately dispatched "itself," like a letter or a post card, using the newly created Room of Time to travel back to where T. Rex was.

Rex was lonely, living in all the agony and pain of having been mean and violent all its days on earth. There would be few on the planet Earth willing to accept a dinosaur, mean or otherwise.

"Let's face it," Mouse said. "The day of the dinosaur is over. You can't be big and brawny and think you can run it all. As for your size, it just gets in the way if you're too big and bossy with people. After all, look at what happened to you, dear friend. Being big and pushy, you just disappeared from the earth. Except for a few old bones in the desert, you're a dead end, friend. That's all. A dead end,

"Well, what can I do?" said Tyrannosaurus Rex. "I do, indeed realize that the earth, today, has no room for a dinosaur. I need you to cut me down to an acceptable size. What can I do? Help me, mouse. Please help me find my way back with the living on earth."

"You are absolutely correct," said Mouse. "You can't be what you were. You can only be what you are, and what you seem to be is an old dinosaur who wants to be back in the swing of things."

"I have an idea. It's a simply marvelous idea; one that will give you, dear Rex, a purposeful meaningful reason to come back into being."

"I could hire you to be my Administrative Aid, friend and butler," Mouse continued. "You could screen all my calls, greet all my guests, and keep me on my invisible toes so I can be prompt for all my appointments. You would be invaluable to me and my work . . ."

"You mean that I, Tyrannosaurus Rex, can once again come among the living and be with all the children, the flowers, the trees, the animals — and you, Magic Mouse? Oh, Mouse. It's a dream come true!"

"Not quite yet," replied Mouse. "There are a few other conditions that must be met."

Rex was stunned. "Other conditions?"

"Yes, old friend. Other conditions. I'm sure you will find them acceptable. They will protect us all from the possibility of your ever becoming violent again."

"You will continue to look like a dinosaur; to be almost as large as you are now. You will be able to think and communicate like a non-violent dinosaur. You will live in Mother Ammal's garden in front of my tree house and there you will interview all who come to see me, for you will be able to talk and communicate with all beings through your thoughts. Only one minor change will be required. If you agree, the deed will be done. Without even knowing what the change was to be, Rex eagerly accepted.

In the batting of an eye, he was in Angelville with Magic Mouse. The great dinosaur, Tyrannosaurus Rex had instantly been converted to the world's only, and very first, talking grape bush tree, exactly in the shape of a great dinosaur!

"MOUSE! What have you DONE to me?!!" Rex bellowed. "A GRAPE BUSH TREE???!! How EMBARRASSING!"

But Mouse gently said, "Don't be silly, old friend. You wanted new life and now you have it. Think, for a moment. You have been reborn without violence. If you were as you had been, you would now, in your anger, be stomping all over the garden, breaking all the flowers. Now, instead, with your legs rooted, you can't hurt anything. Now, as a full fledged grape bush tree, and a speaking one at that.

You will enjoy honor and respect. Though taking up less space, you are now head and shoulders above all the dinosaurs that have ever been. Books will be written about you. The world will stand in awe. Your name, too, will be changed. No longer Tyrannosaurus Rex. You will be called Tyrannosaurus Grape."

The children, hearing Mouse, cheered and formed a dancing circle around the huge grape bush tree shaped like a dinosaur, singing their joyful appreciation for having him among them. Their pure love melted the blanket of fear that had gripped Grape. Though he couldn't join in the dancing, he rustled his leaves and joined the happy singing, harmonizing in a deep bass rumble.

THE BABY SITTER'S MAGIC MOUSE STORY BOOK

The Story of Him

Sir Gawain Dragon and the children arrived at the school early. There was enough time to tell the children a story. It was one he had learned on his timeless search for the holy grail. It was the story of Him, the first human being to ever sit on an elephant's back.

"That's right," said Sir Gawain. "The first being ever. Not a man nor a woman; not a girl or a boy had ever sat on the back of an elephant. It was so far back in time that your grandparents had not been born yet."

"There was a kingdom in that long time ago place where all the people were mean and angry all the time. The name of this Kingdom was Over There. The king of Over There screamed at his generals, who screamed at their colonels, who screamed at their lieutenants, who screamed at their sargents, who screamed at the soldiers, who screamed at the people, who screamed at each other.

Children screamed at their parents and parents screamed at their children. Best friends hit each other just for the fun of it. Husbands and wives were always arguing. There was no peace to be had at all.

The people who had been screamed at were now searching for someone else to scream at. Someone who would not scream back. The people were also looking for someone to hit and kick, who would not hit and kick back. The people searched all the kingdom and finally they found our friend Him. Him, at this point, had no name. No one thought he was worthy enough to have a name. He sat in an obscure corner of the village all day, quietly waving a white cloth. He was always happy, always smiling, always loving. His words were soft and kind. He truly was a joyful being — never angry.

Soon our friend Him was discovered by the angry prople of Over There who were looking for someone to shout at. Word spread rapidly that you could shout at Him, and he wouldn't shout back. You could hit him, and he wouldn't hit back. You could kick him, and he wouldn't kick back.

This went on for a long time . One day, after many years of people shouting at Him, hitting Him, kicking Him, Screaming at Him, Him closed his eyes and prayed. "Dear Lord," he whispered. "Can all this screaming, shouting, hitting and kicking ever stop?"

The Lord came to Him and said, "Get up. Go out in the jungle and find a stick. Then go out and find an elephant. Crawl up behind the elphant and hit it with your stick as hard as you can. Your problem will then be solved."

"But Lord," Him asked. "Must I get violent to end violence?"

"Well," said the Lord, "You've asked for an answer to your prayer and I've given it to you. So go! Find your stick, do as I say, and your problem will be solved."

Him opened his eyes and went into the jungle to do as he had been told. He found a sturdy stick with a good handle, picked it up, and walked on, gently swinging his stick to and fro. He couldn't help thinking how strange it was for Him, a man of peace, to be planning an act of violence.

Suddenly he came upon a giant elephant grazing on banana leaves and tall grass. This was his golden opportunity. He was frightened, but his faith and trust were strong enough to overcome his fear. After all, he thought, how much can my little stick hurt this enormous animal. He snuck up behind the elephant, raised his stick, and was about to bring it down as hard as he could when the elephant turned its giant head and said, "Excuse me, sir, but if you strike me with that stick, I shall step on you and you will be no more.

Him stopped right there, shrinking back meekly as he stuttered an apology—explaining that he had been advised to hit an elephant to end all the violence against himself.

"Good advice," said the elephant. "If you hit me and I step on you, and you are no more, your problem would end indeed, would it not? "

"Hmm. I should have made my prayer clearer," said Him deep in thought. "I wanted to end ALL the violence in Over There."

"I 'm sorry. I can't help you. I can't go stepping on ALL the people," said the elephant. "But you seem to need a friend. I have no friends myself. I would love to have a friend like you.

So Him and the elephant became friends. As they learned of each other's ways, and how best to serve each others needs, the friendship blossomed like a flower in spring, full of joy and deep love.

Meanwhile, in Teenerville, a young elephant lover was ordered by her mother to get rid of all her stuffed animals.

30

The Kingdom of Canine Stray

At the end of a long and dusty road was the tiny Kingdom of Canine Stray. The land had been a gift from a fairy Queen to Fido Rex Ram Rover, making him their first king. For fifteen years, King Fido Rex Ram Rover had spent all his time pitter pattering everywhere, whistling for unwanted dogs to come and live with him. The kingdom of Canine Stray was surrounded by singing trees. They could sing anything they wanted as long as they greeted every morning with "How much is that doggie in the window." King Fido Rex Ram Rover had chosen that song for their anthem so the dogs would no longer feel unwanted.

There was a bone lick bar in the center of the town where any dog could come and bone lick all day long. Next to the bone lick bar, there's a gravy fountain, and next to that, a dog biscuit stand. Next to that is Puppy Playground, with a frisbee throwing and stick fetching park. It had everything a happy dog needed. Well, almost everything.

Every year of our time is seven years for a dog. King Fido Rex Ram Rover was now 85 years old. His little feet were very sore from all that pitter pattering. He needed four new feet very badly, so he went to the swap shop and turned in his worn out old body in exchange for a new puppy one, leaving Canine Stray with no king.

For awhile, the dogs of Canine Stray looked into the eyes of every new puppy, looking for their old friend King Fido Rex Ram Rover. But puppies forget everything. King Fido Rex Ram Rover had changed his looks, and even he didn't know who he was, so how could anyone ever find him? The dogs of Canine Stray could only never forget his kindness to them.

Puppies are too young for kinging, of course, so the old dogs of Canine Stray sent a delegation to Angelville to offer their crown to Magic Mouse's friend, Donald McDougal Hound, known as Grand Tailwagger of Planet Earth.

At first Donald McDougal Hound was afraid he could never fill the paws of old King Fido Rex Ram Rover, but the delegation explained that the dogs of Canine Stray had chosen him because they wanted the same laws that were obeyed in the town of Angelville, and he would be most able to know them all.

Donald McDougal Hound knew the laws of Angelville very well. They were very simple. Anyone could do whatever he wanted as long as he was careful to never hurt a single living thing in any way.

Donald McDougal Hound sent a thought message to his friend Magic Mouse. who knew that Donald McDougal Hound did not want to leave his friends. Magic Mouse then assured his friend that he could stay and rule from Angelville; that he could set up an embassy in the Kingdom of Canine Stray, appoint a Baron of Dish Cleaning, a Marquis of Scrap Eating and a Band of Knights of Bone Buryers to help him, and he could just fly back and forth on the court's magic carpets

All the plants, flowers , trees, animals and children of Angelville were proud and honored to know Donald McDougal Hound. Not one citizen objected to his accepting the crown of Canine Stray, so he accepted. On arriving in Canine Stray, Donald McDougal Hound was quickly crowned their king by his happy subjects, who were ever so delighted to be a sister state with Angelville.

Runaway Poochie

When Runaway Jones ran away from home, he left behind everyone who loved him. Nobody loved runaway Jones before he ran away from home, so that left nobody.

That's what Runaway Jones thought.

What Runaway Jones didn't know was that Poochie, the dog next door, loved him. The reason Poochie loved Runaway Jones was that she, too, had no one who loved her. No one ever even paid attention to her— except for Runaway Jones, who would sometimes tickle her belly and call her Poochie Koochie.

After Runaway Jones ran away from home, Poochie missed him so much that she decided to go look for him. The next time the pizza man came to deliver a pizza, Poochie was waiting for him. The minute he started to open the gate, she was ready to scoot through the opening, and the pizza man was left with one hand carrying the pizza, and the other hand stuck on the gate. That's how Poochie got the name Runaway Poochie. As she had never had been outside the gate before, everything was new to her. All she had to help her find Runaway Jones was the memory of his smell that was like nobody else's smell.

Since no one had ever loved him enough to bathe him, and he had never learned to bathe himself, his smell was very easy to follow. In no time Runaway Poochie found a piece of his pain where he had dropped it. She also found the smell of a bigger pain that he had picked up in its place, so she had something stronger to follow. Each time she found where he had dropped a piece of the new pain, there was the smell of a bigger new pain that took its place.

By then the stink of the pain he was carrying was so bad it out smelled all the smell that Runaway Jones had taken with him. Runaway Poochie had to start asking strangers if they had seen Runaway Jones. Because Poochie was a dog, everyone thought it was another dog she was looking for, so they suggested that she look for him in the Kingdom of Canine Stray.

Poochie had no idea of where to look for the Kingdom of Canine Stray. When she asked directions, everyone told her to follow her nose. She had a very twitchy nose, so her nose led her this way and that. Now that she was a stray herself, she finally found the long dusty road that led to Canine Stray. It just happened to be the day Angelville was the visiting team and their star player was Runaway Jones.

She tried to run up to him when she found him, but she was so tired, all she could do was crawl. When Runaway Jones saw her, her hair was so dirty and tangled, he had to turn her over on her back before he could recognize her belly.

"POOCHIE, KOOCHIE!" he cried,"

And he started to tickle her little belly button. Poochie wearily wiggled her tail, too tired to wag it, just to let him know how happy she was. Nothing is ever happier in this world than a loveless one finding a loved one.

Because love loves love.

35

Puppy School

It was, as usual, a peaceful and serene morning in Angelville. The children had just finished breakfast at granny Mable's Stew Pot, and were in the garden hugging the trees, blowing kisses to the flowers, and smiling up at the cotton candy clouds overhead. Magic Mouse was at the stick ball course, watching the visiting team from the Kingdom of Canine Stray playing the home team. They were playing visiting team rules because that was the polite thing to do with guests. The Canine Stray team used tails instead of sticks. Only three of the Angelville players had tails, so most of the home team was sitting on the bench. It didn't matter that the visiting team had so many more players than the visitors. Nobody kept score. The winner was the one who could lose the most balls and still not cry about it.

The children wanted to play with the puppies who were supposed to come with the visitors, but because it was such a nice day, the puppies had stayed behind to study their stick fetching instead. When the children heard this, they all decided to go back with the visiting team after the game so they could sign up for courses that were not taught in Angelville. Magic Mouse was pleased that the children wanted to learn. It didn't take long. Bozo the tramp dog was the winner, losing all the balls they had, hitting a string of foul balls with his shaggy tail. He was duly humble as he hid his pride, thanking the mayor over and over for the bronze broom award.

The Kingdom of Canine Stray was famous for their Pet Rock workshops. Anyone from Canine Stray could pick up any rock from anywhere and tell you the name, what it was made of, what it was good for, how it served Nature, and how it was able to go around anyone at whom it was thrown. Each rock had its own trick, and learning their tricks came in handy for any one who wanted to go around trouble.

The Seeing Eye classes for seeing people to take care of blind dogs was also very popular, but best of all was the special stick fetching training that could only be had in Canine Stray. The children were most anxious to learn how to get back the sticks that the stick throwers kept throwing away in Angelville.

While they waited for the players to finish their game, they studied the ways in which each dog swung his tail to hit the ball. Since anyone might grow a tail, one never could tell when the lessons might be useful.

Bozo was very happy to show off his bronze broom as he swept a path for the others on the long dusty road that led to the Kingdom of Canine Stray. When they got to the stick fetching range, King Donald McDougal was waiting for them, glad of the chance to repay the people of Angelville for all the balls Bozo had lost, by supplying the visitors with as many sticks as they could carry. As the children found the sticks getting heavier and heavier on the way home, they were slowly dropped, one by one, so that the puppies of Canine Stray, following them, were the ones who got most of the stick fetching training. It was a very nice day. Long after it was over, many of the children of Angelville could be seen trying to learn to hit pet rocks with false tails pinned to their back pockets.

It's rumored that even Magic Mouse did some practicing with his real tail, although nobody could see him doing it.

38

Rin Tin Tinny Dollar Bill

Rin Tin Tinny dollar bill was so dog eared that he was adopted by the dogs of the Kingdom of Canine Stray as one of them.

As a dog, Rin Tin Tinny Dollar Bill, called "Rin" for shot, always tried to be one of man's best friends Most people loved Rin every bit as much as they loved their dogs — even more, perhaps— especially when he bought food for his master instead of waiting for his master to buy a dog biscuit for HIM.

The children of Angelville weren't sure they wanted to play with Rin. He was dogged by the saying that money is the Root of All Evil. And money was what Rin Tin Tinny Dollar Bill had been in real life. The children had heard people were always fighting over money, and the children of Angelville wanted nothing to do with any fighting. So they went to Magic Mouse for advice.

"There IS play money that you can play with," said Mouse. "but Rin Tin Tinny Dollar Bill is a REAL dollar bill. If you play with Rin Tin Tinny Dollar Bill, you may lose him and you'll never see him again." The children listened to Mouse and decided not to play with real money.

Rin was lonely when no one would pay with him, so he went to Magic Mouse. "Help me, Magic Mouse," he begged. (As a dog he had learned how to beg.) "Please help me get out of being the Root of All Evil!"

"Well, THAT IS WRONG," said Mouse. "You are NOT EVIL. Money is what keeps PEACE in the Market Place. Without money, every one would be fighting over what one should give for what one wants to get. Like say— if Apple Tree has lot of apples, and Chicken Little has one egg, how would they agree on a trade? Chicken Little will want six apples –(that is half a dozen)– because Apple Tree has so many, and she must have six apples in case two of them are rotten. Then Apple Tree will say "okay, but, what if your one egg is rotten? You will have four of my apples, and I will not have ANYthing!"

" Without money, they would fight all day. If you promise not to steal away from the children, I will tell you what to say" said Magic Mouse. Rin Tin Tinny Dollar Bill agreed not to get lost, and Mouse taught him to say, "Look. Chicken Little must give ME to Apple Tree for FOUR apples. Apple Tree will cut me into four quarters and give Chicken Little one quarter for her one egg. If two of the apples are rotten, Chicken will still have two good apples. And if the egg is rotten, Apple Tree will still have three quarters."

Then Rin Tin Tinny Dollar Bill broke himself up into a hundred pennies, and taught the children how to play penny ante with him.

And to thank Magic Mouse, he went to the King of the Kingdom of Canine Stray and had himself printed a million times, so every one could have a way to measure value in the market place.

41

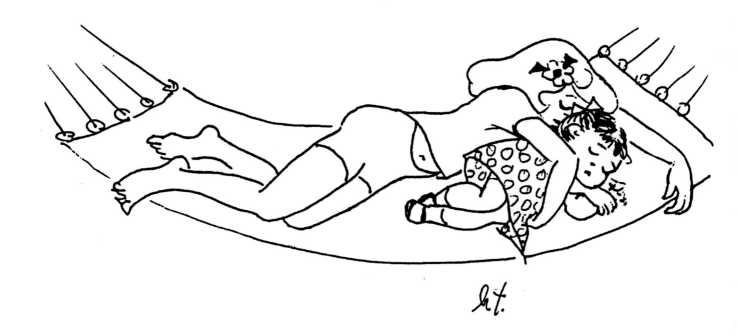

The 8 Henderson Place Foundation, Inc., the d'Alessio's institutionalized home overflowing with the century's accumulation of archives, is launching a
WEB SITE CEMETERY IN CYBERSPACE.

Back in the '70s, when artists were burning their unsold paintings to protect heirs from the tax on their value "when the artist dies", the 8 Henderson Place Foundation bought two lots in Nevada in which to create an art cemetery in the desert.
Better the art should be buried than burnt.

The project was dropped when the tax law was reformed. Rembrandt, after all — died in the poorhouse with no idea of what dealers might some day receive for his works. As the population exploded. As small apartments began running out of wall space; as shelving for the ever increasing production of books and magazines began overflowing to the street for rubish pickup, the foundation held onto the lots. And the dream. While continuing the open house activities for which the house was accustomed, the accumulating archives began serving as insulation piled against the walls. After Greg died, his widow, (hilda terry d'Alessio) turned over the house to the Foundation to simplify the continuity. As soon as the deed was transferred, the insurance company canceled.
With no coverage, all in-house programs had to be discontinued.

Fortunately, with a half dozen computers at hand, and plenty of talent to operate them, the foundation was well prepared to "get out of the house" — to create the dreamed of art cemetery in *CYBERSPACE.*

For no reason other than the fact that Mrs. d'Alessio was now a bouncing 88, June 2002 was designated "Hilda Terry Month" by the Friends of Lulu *(women cartooniists).*
Hilda had created a book illustrating the stories of an old friend with her old comic strips from the 50s. The friend died and so did the book. As everyone was doing things with and for her, a fellow artist rescued the book, scanned it, and gave her a thousand CDs for the foundation.
The Baby Sitters Magic Mouse Story Book, remembering Harvey Job Matusow, introduces the first memorial in an 8 Henderson Place Foundation program to create and maintain cemeteries of forgotten creative keepsakes for posterity. For information on who, what and where — and how you, too, can join the move to this New Age storage facility for precious treasures, go to
www.8hendersonplace.org

UNFORGETTABLE HAS-BEENS
by Hilda terry

As radio and television began taking over the news, and revenues for papers and magazines dropped below the growing demand of workers, cartoonists found themselves scrambling for other remunerative outlets. Greg turned to painting, and I turned our first floor into an Art Gallery. Matusow had become an artist during his jail sentence, and was creating a monthly art calendar. I was doing his typing in exchange for free ads. He picked up a Varityper, and as I learned to operate it, he got this wonderful idea for an Art Collector's Almanac. If you do a review of every artist who has an exhibition in New York, he figured, you'd cover every artist worthy of recognition. We soon realized the varityper was wrong for a book on Art. I took it and had a trade...cold type, warm heart...until I found my next career, but a lot of unemployed artists loved the idea. With a bunch of volunteers and a little financial help, he finally produced one issue of what is aptly described in Brian O'Doherty's review. The whole effort was so precarious from one day to the next, we all got to be life-long friends. In fact, Matusow adopted me as his mother and for the rest of his life, as long as he was in the country, he called me like a dutiful son, every two weeks.

When he wanted me to illustrate his Magic Mouse stories, in which the mouse is too small to be seen, I saw how I could use the Dorcas cartoons from the 50s. This is the book. I had given Matusow my American Express number to buy CDs for Xmas. It was the first time in his life that he had ever had a credit card. He got carried away with the magic of it, transferring every day or two, a thousand or two thousand from my credit to his Gandhi Peace Center. He thought he was going to get rich and put it back. He didn't know I would have to come up with the full amount at the end of the month. When he realized what he had done to me, he promised to sell the book to a hotel chain to get me out of that mess.

He had an accident and died. I'm still paying interest on the money I had to borrow to take care of American Express. He died knowing he owed me. After Dorcas had found the way to get into my head, she must've started showing others the way. Every time someone close to me dies suddenly, leaving something undone, they get to me and I never know what it is that they need from me until after I've taken care of it for them.

The experience with Bob Roston in 1980 was the first of a series of similar experiences. Since Bob, it's been one crazy thing after another.

Before he passed, Matusow borrowed $2,000 from someone else to help me with the interest. He is now VERY DEFINITELY up there trying to help me. He helped us get rid of a squatter who told the police she was a legal tenant paying $1,000 a month. The law gave her the right to lock US out of OUR space. We are totally recovered from her deterrence and are back on track. This book is the springboard for a year of ambitious new exhibitions, renewed internet activity, and reorganization.

If you are reading this book, we very much appreciate your help.

Remembering Harvey Job Matusow 1926-2002

Harvey Marshall Matusow was born October 3 1926 in Brooklyn, New York. Harvey later went by the name Marshall, and still later, Harvey Job Matusow, or just Job Matusow. He died June 30 from complications following an automobile accident in January, 2002.

He lived an incredible life. He saw the Hindenberg crash as a child. He was outside the signing of the Armistice Treaties ending World War II. Matusow was in the prison cell next to psychologist and inventor Willhelm Reich when Reich died. He encouraged his friend Yoko Ono to come to London where she met John Lennon. As an out of work actor he delivered TV sets in NYC with Steve McQueen and other future movie stars. He worked in advertising as a contemporary of Andy Warhol before Warhol left the business to pursue his arts career. Having served in World War II, he was invited to the White House by Lyndon Johnson for his exploits.

Worked for the FBI and Senator Joe MacCarthy in U.S. anti-communist hearings. Wrote a best selling book, "FALSE WITNESS", where he recanted his testimony—for which he served time in prison convicted of perjury *(not on the stand, but in the BOOK)*—bringing down MacCarthy and his red scare machine.

Was involved in stand up comedy, childrens radio programs, TV, journalism, underground magazines and newspapers, avant garde music, taken vows of poverty, released seven albums, and produced cable TV programming for the Mormon community. He spent much of his life volunteering and helping prostitutes, indian reservations and developmentally disabled children. Has also been a professional clown and a successful toy inventor. Toured with a band of bell ringers. Once had a garden with plants growing out of a bevy of discarded pianos. Ran the only public access TV service in Utah, SCAT-TV.

Job was writing his sixth book, The Stringless Yo Yo, an autobiography covering his entire life story. He is survived by his 11th wife, Irene, whom he married in November of 2001, and by his children and adopted children, grand-children, other ex-wives and too many close friends to possibly mention here.

A number of web-sites maintained by them—(search for Job Matusow)—continue to carry on some of his work in progress—and his final legacy, the Gandhi Peace Centre in Utah. Related sites sharing his books, music, and other works are found at **www.magicmouse.org** and **www.beastofbusiness.com.**

Mal Humes is producing a video documentary on Harvey Job Matusow and welcomes the opportunity to do interviews with people who knew Matusow at various periods of his life. Please feel free to email stories to mal2@MAL.NET, or mail videotapes of you talking about his impact on your life to Mal Humes, PO BOX 8, KERNERSVILLE, NC 27285-0008. Ask Humes for his 8 page bio/obit website.

While producing an Arts Calendar in the 60s, Harvey (then Marshall)—with a couple bucks in his pocket— undertook to produce an annual Art Collectors Almanac. As one of his helpful gang of volunteers, I was a participant in the final triumph of coming out with one issue, an adventurous emotional roller coaster ride from start to finish resulting in a lifetime friendship.

When he asked me to illustrate a revival of his Magic Mouse stories, I saw it as an opportunity to try something innovative. We created an ice breaker for babysitters, a book generating a teaching relationship and exposing pre-readers to the fun of reading comics.

hilda terry

The Art Collector's Almanac

No **1**

1965

BY MARSHALL MATUSOW

Associate Editors: *Hilda Terry*
Lucille Whiting
Leonard Horowitz
Paul Cummings
Eline Mc Knight
Aaron Cohen
Corine Robbins
Cecile Ruchin

JEROME E. TREISMAN, Publisher
ROBERT SCHWARTZ, Associate Publisher

ART COLLECTOR'S ALMANAC Inc.   110 East 10th Street   Huntington Station, Long Island 11746

INTRODUCTION BY BRIAN O'DOHERTY

The *fact* of this book, the five-pound, two-inch-thick physical presence of it, is a form of evidence, a weighty Bible to swear by. What is sworn depends on the prejudice of the witness. These 700 pages provide more evidence for the quantitative clerks of the cultural explosion. They are muscle to persuade gallery investors. They document exhaustively that the New York scene is the most active anywhere just now. Like any system of fact and statistics, they can be bent to any point of view. In the next few years, this book will be used to prove virtually anything. Which is to say it is a major, distinguished bit of work.

Here for the first time has been built the factual coal-face, glistening and solid, from which the historian will extract the ores, trace veins and trends. This book offers the living substance from which cultural history is mined and written.

Lastly, this volume is the most steady monument to date to the quicksilver life of one Harvey Marshall Matusow, whose picaresque adventures — economic, esthetic, and social — have made him many reputations, to which is now added one as lexicographer. His "Art Collector's Almanac" is the ultimate one-man show.

"Where did Jackson Pollock have his first exhibition?" said someone at the Chuck Wagon on 8th Street (where the abstract expressionists used to go after the Cedar Street Bar shut down). Matusow doesn't remember who said it. It could have been Landes Lewitin or Leonard Horowitz or anyone you meet in the bars, coffee houses, backrooms of what is vaguely called The Scene. But the point is no one knew the answer, presumably a date and location as important to American cultural history as 1066 to the English.

The mythology of the New York School is gradually devouring the facts on which it is based. "The art world" says Matusow, "is so anarchistic by its nature that there is no single source, no way people can get facts—art history majors, artists, museum directors. Take baseball, for example. If you want to find out what a player did in a poney league game on July 14th in 1926 in the 3rd inning, you can check it out in a comprehensive record book in any library. It's the same for theater, films. There isn't a field in which there is popular interest that hasn't got some kind of detached factual record."

The uses, abuses and pleasures to which this book can be put are obvious. One however, is missing. In imaginative pursuit of the "profile" of the American artist, Matusow related 7500 birth dates to the Zodiac, discovered that 563 were Cancer. Quickly he mobilized 3 groups of 2000 each—writers, actors and actresses, politicians, plus a huge group from the general population. He discovered there was no difference. Most people are Cancer anyway. But some of the remaining facts offer plentiful opportunity for play. The fact that the average age of last season's exhibitor was —, that it was more male than female, more living than dead is not likely to serve any conceivable practical purpose except for sidebets in a game of Trivia in 1984. But the hard areas of this factual organism are invaluable.

The pedigrees—1400 of them—from Aach to Zox (page 81) compose a reference library of virtually every important—and unimportant—artist or sculptor on the New York scene. The bibliography of reviews, articles, and illustrations provides the first easily accessible base for writers, reseachers, historians. The galleries and museums section (page 503) contain the first informed and reputable guide to their policies. It has been needed for years, especially by slide-bearing aspirants in search of The Word.

The basic idea demanded two things that the lexicographer had—a majesty of concept that safer people would call foolhardy, and impolite people mad; and a caloric energy drawing on a brutal stamina, a cheerful persistence, a manic dash. When I first met Matusow he was at a desk at the New York Times, taking down the season's details with a pencil on a yellow pad. When he told me what he was doing, it sounded as if he were working out a one-man system of pulleys to raise Abu Simbel. Now he has done it, and the results, majestic and slightly flawed, back up this foreword with an obvious moral.

For it was not a Foundation, too often the polished subsidizer of the uninspired civil service of the arts, that midwifed this book. Nor was it the commission of a fat cat publishing house putting its money on a reference book winner. It was a single person's persistently realized impulse that—like the artist's—had elements of compulsion, vision, foolhardiness or whatever you want to call it.

Now that it has been done this volume will either be the first of a great series, or it will remain a solitary phenomenon, a permanent rebuke to a community that did not deserve it.

THE SALEM FIRE

Joe Aronson, Newburyport's harried telegraph operator rose from his dit-dit-dada-dit, stretching his neck to look over the soot covered heads of the desperate refugees crowding his depot. The brother-in-law of his sister was excitedly waving from the doorway, shouting "ANNIE HAD A GIRL!!". Soberly jerking his head, acknowledging the message, Joe quickly returned to the crowd clamoring for his attention.

Salem was burning. Burned out of their homes, Salemites fleeing the fire were crowding the trains, running to neighboring towns where they might find relief with family or friends. The telephone had been invented, but few could as yet afford the dollar a month service fee. Joe and the other telegraph operators along the rail line were the only means of communication.

Eager to be helpful, gangs of kids were showing up at the depots to volunteer as couriers. People were getting in touch. Tempted to join them; to be part of the frenetic activity, the new "uncle" hesitated for a moment before racing down Merrimac Street to bring his news to the rest of the relatives in the small town's interrelated Jewish/Armenian community.

As every train entered the depot, Joe left his post to look for his parents among the passengers. Finally he saw them standing on the platform of the last car of the last arrival. His father, with the help of the mother who wouldn't let go, was unloading a Singer sewing machine. The sewing machine and her husband's best suit were all she had managed to save from the fire. In the park, their first sanctuary in their flight, they had run into a neighbor who had fled in his longies. She had given him her husband's suit. Now all these two soot covered refugees had left in this world was the sewing machine.

Joe wanted to take his parents to his apartment across from the depot where his wife, had prepared a bed on the living room floor, but learning of the baby's arrival, the new life came first. Loading the sewing machine on one of the carts whose drivers had also rushed to the depot to help, the sooty couple ran to their daughter. Annie Fellman, nee Aronson, had been warned that giving birth would be no picnic. No one had warned her, however, of the possibility that she would open her eyes to see her mother hidden from top to bottom behind a sooty black mist, hanging onto an equally sooty sewing machine.

My grandmother was finally persuaded to let go, to clean herself up so she could hold the baby, and there the machine stayed waiting to become mine. Before I was old enough to go to school, I was standing in front of that thing, one foot pedaling like mad, cautious fingers safely guiding small rags through the plunging mechanism to come out BIG rags.

By the time I was 5, the house on 20 Prescott Street, Salem Mass., had been rebuilt. I would spend my summers with my Salem grandparents, and the cousins who lived downstairs. The highlight, for us, was always the Firemen's Muster commemorating the Salem Fire. At first there was only one motorized fire engine in the parade, but year after year there would be fewer and fewer horse drawn wagons until they were a thing of the past.

Occasionally someone would call the fire "the witches' revenge," commenting on the screaming burning cat that was said to have carried the fire from house to house. It was just a joke. The immigrants settling New England at the beginning of the century had no interest in Salem's ancient history. When asked about my birthday, I used to say, "You know Salem where they burnt the witches? Well, the day I was born, they burnt Salem." That, too, was said in jest.

My birth, June 25, 1914 is registered in Newburyport's city hall as Theresa Hilda Fellman. Carved on my stone waiting for me at the foot of the hill in the Hebrew Cemetery in Salisbury, Mass., inviting you to "sit, sit" you'll find me as Tryna Hyuda, (in Hebrew) the great grandmother for whom I was named.

REMEMBERING DORCAS GOOD by HILDA TERRY

We didn't know any artists. Maybe there weren't any. A little Greek boy and I were the only artists in Newburyport. In Salem, there was a mailman next door to my grandparents who had 6 sons. The oldest was my uncle Eddie's age. They went to dances together and came home with all the cups. I used to sign my drawings, "drawn by the niece of the champion Charleston Dancer of New England."

The youngest was my brother's age. They had tin cans with string strung from our house to their's over which the boys hollered. Somewhere in between, there was one who was an artist. To our knowledge Al Robley and I were the only artists in Salem.

When radio was first invented. I got a job at Hygrade, Peabody's radio tube factory, where I acquired an interest in electronics, science, and puzzles. When, in 1931, I realized I had not grown up to be the artist everyone had expected, I packed my shoes in a brown paper bag, put one dress on top of another, and took a bus to New York where I knew there'd be a lot of artists.

I found my artists, registered with two art schools, got a job in Schraffts, 1 meal a day, $3 a week, later raised to $5, and tips. Found the garment district and began free-lancing.

Everyone knew I wanted to be a cartoonist. I caricatured the Stylish Stouts. I even created a fashion comic in one of the little magazines I set up.

Artists who had lofts in the village would have rent parties, 10 cents admission for people from Brooklyn and the Bronx to come and mingle with the artists, poets, and writers. The latter had to be lured to be there for the minglers, so someone said, "Come down Friday night. A friend is coming who just sold a cartoon to Esquire." We got married in 1938.

My husband, Greg, was a good teacher. He wouldn't let me go out with anything that would embarrass him until he saw I had something. "Try it." He said. I took it out and sold the New Yorker, College Humor and the Saturday Evening Post with my first venture. I don't think that's EVER been done before or since.

A few years later, King Features called me in and showed me a telegram from Wm. Randolph Hearst. "GET HILDA TERRY," it said. My comic strip "It's A Girl's Life" made its debut December 7, 1941.

When one of my imitators thoughtlessly named his character Penny, the same as mine, I took advantage of the opportunity to redraw my characters, reformat and rename the strip TEENA. It ran all over the world until the newspaper strike of 1963. The Boston Globe got it in their package, but never published it. My family and friends never got to see my work. **That was strange.** They HAD it ... and they never used it.

Another strange thing I did not notice at the time was a 4/5 year old character that had a life of her own in this strip about teenagers.

After Teena, I hit the unemployable age and began free-lancing... anything I was asked to do. If I didn't know how to do it, I ran to the library and found out how. Among 10 other things, I was doing engineering drawings for inventor's patent applications. If you're drawing something that does not exist, the inventor must explain exactly what's going to make it work. That was my college education.

After the Astrodome was built, they were looking for a cartoonist who understood the computer. There I was. I had a real fun career in baseball pioneering computer generated graphics for electronic scoreboards, from here to China, 1969 to 1986.

A man from Boston Whose job it was to shop for a scoreboard came and sat beside me at the Royals opening. I sold him our board. My family and friends were elated. Finally, they could be proud of me.

But management announced there'd be none of this cartoon gimikry in Fenway Park and AGAIN, I'm doing this fantastic work everywhere but not where family and friends can see it. **STRANGER yet.** They BOUGHT the board on which they could DO all these things, and NEVER USED my programs.

In my 65th year, I began to realize SOME one was HELPING me. And it wasn't God. In my National Cartoonists Society bio written in 1978, I am still joking about the Salem Fire. In 1979 I was doing the kooky things trying to reach my invisible collaborator. I wound up with a child crying MA-MA for a woman being tried for witchcraft. Asked if she was my guardian angel, the tangled hair shook. Negative. A dirty hand gestured back and forth indicating she and I were one. Hey! A past life? Asked her name, she lifted her tunic and MOONED at me.

Asked how she happened to be me, she said "Rebecca," Actually, we never spoke. She pulled words out of my head and highlighted them. "Rebecca your mother?" I asked. Shaking her head "no" again, she brought up 3 words, Grandmother, Rebecca, Nurse.

MY grandmother's name was Rivka. Russian for Rebecca. And I had lived with her through my first years. You could say she nursed me. I assumed she was naming MY grandmother. It didn't make sense. My grandmother was alive in 1914.

Clearly, my head was playing games with me. Still ? ? ?

"Don't discuss this with anyone," my husband cautioned. "They'll think you're nuts." I tried one night with one of the talk shows. My husband was right. Anyway, I didn't know what to make of it. I put it behind me.

One day I picked up a book called The Devil In Massachusetts expecting another one of those horror things. It turned out to be based on some WPA research on the witch trials. I thumbed through it looking for any witches who may have had children. There she was. DORCAS GOOD, daughter of Sarah and William Good. I never knew anyone named Dorcas. She couldn't find the name in my head so she gave me the little Torchas... a "sounds like".

Greg got his wish, in 1993, for an age divisible by 11, just before he would've overshot. Every year, from where he is, he remembers my birthday with a miracle. I have his job, and I have his social security which is better than mine. He's taking such good care of me, I now understand that a lesser God must have been taking care of me all along. Maybe I have a BUNCH of Guardian Angels.

I noticed the 4 numbers Dorcas had given me were all rearrangements of the same digits. One, 1687, was the year when she must've been born. AND there was a REBECCA NURSE in the book ...a grandmother of many ... my first encounter with the name.

By the time New England began planning the 300th Anniversary of the Witch trials, I had written the Chamber of Commerce and the Salem Librarian for the WPA research on Dorcas Good. Living in New York, pursuing a very busy life of my own, I had no interest in what was going on back home. I had not seen Arthur Miller's play, the Crucible. I now stumbled on a copy of the book in a sidewalk stall. Reading it, I was struck by the inconsistency of his version of the mother. One thing I knew, from our brief encounters, was that Dorcas LOVED the woman who had been her mother.

I also knew that far from cravenly trying to use her pregnancy to save her life, she had actually COACHED the child to give evidence against herself in the hope that by confessing to the mother's guilt, the child's life would be spared.

My mother had saved all my cartoons in her garage. I found them after she died and took them home with me. They were beginning to fall apart so I laminated them, rescuing them just in time.

Going through them half a century after their creation was like someone else had done them. Looking at them now, objectively, I realized that child had put herself in my comic strip! **SHE** was my mysterious helper. Watching me relive MY lost adolescence in my cartoons, DORCAS must have learned to do the same. Here she was reliving the lost sane year of HER childhood.

THIS foundation was created in the 70s to preserve the history of the 21 designated NYC landmark houses at the entrance to Carl Schurz Park. Our house, being the largest in the alley, had been designated the repository for the archives, memorabilia and other records. As these grew, taking over the whole house, we had promised to leave the house to the foundation so it can stay here.

I came back after 20 tears of running all over the country. All the old neighbors were gone. The foundation was on hold. Finding myself the last of the founders, I could have turned the archives over to another organization, sold the house, and retired to Florida. I was 78. I just couldn't do that. Never thought of it for a minute.

I was going to start this UNFORGETTABLE HAS-BEENS with Satchel Paige. I interviewed him about putting him on the scoreboard. He said "If Ewing Kauffman wants me on his scoreboard, he's gotta PAAAAAY me."   I looked him up and found he is VERY MUCH remembered.

Since someone had scanned this book and given the foundation 1,000 CDs, I saw I could use it with the infamous MATUSOW as the unforgettable has-been. Then we went to Kansas City where I thought I was gonna steal the show. Turns out *I* am the unforgettable has-been. The Foundation has 150 CARTOONS AGAINST THE AXIS, collected in 1942. We've photographed them for digital reproduction, and have arranged a MoCCA exhibition for this winter. HOW, as a forgotten has-been, am I gonna promote this?

A couple of my students of 10 years ago, having gone into film making, just came back to do a documentary on me. As part of their effort, they took me back to Salem. My life has been so filled with miracles ... OR ... coincidences, I never know which. I DO know they can't ALL be coincidences. We visited the Rebecca Nurse Home in Danvers. At one point I realized Rebecca Nurse could be my guardian angel. To her, I am still Dorcas. But I am NOT Dorcas.

I have had my OWN life. I have a whole raft of friends of my own in the next world. I don't know if Dorcas Good is my past life, but she HAS been something in my PRESENT life. And Rebecca did arrange this trip. I was overwhelmed with the sense of her presence...an intense urgency.

Rebecca never carried to her grave what was done to her. She was too outraged over what they had done to this 5 year old child. Dorcas was mentally unbalanced for the rest of her life.

When we "go home," we leave all our physical handicaps behind. In the Infinite world, past, present and future must exist simultaneously, as in the hard disk. Time is meaningless. Rebecca must have waited for her. Rebecca must have been helping Dorcas, teaching her the other world knowledge, preparing her for her reentry. It was probably Rebecca's idea for her to become a cartoonist when it was hardly recognized as a female occupation. Nothing beats laughter for healing a battered soul.

Through me, she has had a life that made up for the last one. To the extent that we share one mind, she learns what I learn. And what she knows, I know … so many things *I* have no way of knowing otherwise

With all that I now knew, I was compelled to write a book about my experience with Dorcas for the 300th anniversary of the witch trials. NOOOObody was interested. Even my Newburyport bookstore refused to take any on consignment.

I self published 500 copies, and gave them away. My **THIRD** mysterious rejection. I suspect the mystery is solved.

I'm trying to set up internet marketing so the foundation can support itself after I'm gone. I'm wondering what kind of products they can sell. I am now 90. I don't have much time left.

The Rebecca Nurse home has ALL the products for our purpose! We have to make a deal with them. The New England market is THEIRS. Was Rebecca behind the strange rejections? Making it clear, she is not going to let me intrude on that?

Would you ever guess that a guardian angel in our simple concept of Heaven might be this sophisticated about the economy in OUR world? We're counting the galaxies in the Universe, Next we'll be counting the universes in a cosmic sea of Universes. I have a pill the size of a tiny pearl in which they claim a billion live bacteria, each with its own complicated life system. What do we know. Maybe souls in the immortal world are like us because they ARE us.

Dorcas is not a has-been, but this *IS HER BOOK*. The 20 odd cartoons you can print out with the CD are my drawings, but **HER IDEAS.** How often do we have a chance to peek into the mind of what may be a ghost in the vastness of a very complex system in which we find ourselves?

See my website. www.hildaterry.com

We can't explain what neither of us understands, but Dorcas is, as far as I'm concerned, the entity who came into this world with me … perhaps with her first breath of our atmosphere. She is definitely herself from another world, with perhaps a vague memory of the Dorcas she once was in this world. In her persistent claim that she once was a little birdie, there seems a remnant of her memory of her damaging testimony that her mother's familiars were three birds, a yellow one and a black one. She was too young to know numbers. She just remembered what her mother, in her effort to save her daughter's life, had coached her to say.

One day, in a Dorcas mood, I let her take over as she seemed to have, in her own mind, what she wanted to draw. Interesting that she seems to have read Doonsbury, maybe over my shoulder, through MY eyes. She dictated a cartoon of ME. Here are a few.

During the 300th commemoration, someone sent me a video of a reenactment. There was a brief scene of Dorcas and Rebecca Nurse, huddling together. No dialogue, but the face of the child, playing the role of the littlest witch, was the same face I had drawn for Gwendolyn.

DOOMSBURG (Salem, Mass. 1692)

with apologies to Garry Trudeau

Printed in the United States
By Bookmasters